MW00622443

THE MOST OF IT

BOOKS BY MARY RUEFLE

Indeed I Was Pleased With the World

A Little White Shadow

Throughout

Tristimania

Apparition Hill

Among the Musk Ox People

Post Meridian

Cold Pluto

The Adamant

Life Without Speaking

Memling's Veil

THE MOST OF IT

MARY RUEFLE

WAVE BOOKS

SEATTLE/NEW YORK

Published by Wave Books
www.wavepoetry.com

Wave Books titles are distributed to the trade by
Consortium Book Sales and Distribution
Phone: 800-283-3572 / SAN 631-760X

Library of Congress Cataloging-in-Publication Data:

Ruefle, Mary, 1952-

The most of it / Mary Ruefle. -- 1st ed.

p. cm.

ISBN 978-1-933517-30-8 (trade cloth : alk. paper) -- ISBN

978-1-933517-29-2 (trade paper : alk. paper)

I. Title.

PS3568.U36M67 2008

813'.54--dc22

2007041633

Designed and composed by Milan Bozic
Printed in the United States of America

9 8 7 6 5 4 3 2 1

FIRST EDITION

Wave Books 014

TO YOU

CONTENTS

Hardly had we entered the cemetery when we lost one another. The trees that had pushed up between the graves blocked our view, and our shouts went unanswered. And then, just as suddenly, we found one another again . . .

—TZVETAN TODOROV

SNOW

Every time it starts to snow, I would like to have sex. No matter if it is snowing lightly and unseriously, or snowing very seriously, well on into the night, I would like to stop whatever manifestation of life I am engaged in and have sex, with the same person, who also sees the snow and heeds it, who might have to leave an office or meeting, or some arduous physical task, or, conceivably, leave off having sex with another person, and go in the snow to me, who is already, in the snow, beginning to have sex in my snow-mind. Someone for whom, like me, this is an ultimatum, the snow sign, an ultimatum of joy, though as an ultimatum beyond joy as well as sorrow. I would like to be in the classroom — for I am a teacher — and closing my book stand up, saying "It is snowing and I must go have sex, good-bye," and walk out of the room. And starting my car, in the beginning stages of snow, know that he is starting his car, with the flakes falling on its windshield, or, if he is at home, he is looking at the snow and knowing I will arrive, snowy, in ten or twenty or thirty minutes, and, if the snow has stopped off, we, as humans, can make a decision, but not while it is still snowing, and even half-snow would be something to be obeyed. I often wonder where the birds go in a snowstorm, for they disappear completely. I always think of them deep inside the bushes, and further along inside the trees and deep inside of the forests, on branches where no snow can reach, deeply recessed for the time of the snow, not oblivious to it, but intensely accepting their incapacity, and so enduring the snow in brave little inborn ways, with their feathered heads bowed down for warmth. Wings, the mark of a bird, are quite useless in snow. When I am inside having sex while it snows I want to be thinking about the birds too, and I want my love to love thinking about the birds as much as I do, for it is snowing and we are having sex under or on top of the blankets and the birds cannot be that far away, deep in the stillness and silence of the snow, their breasts still have color, their hearts are beating, they breathe in and out while it snows all around them, though thinking about the birds is not as fascinating as watching it snow on a cemetery, on graves and tombstones and the vaults of the dead, I love watching it snow on graves, how cold the snow is, even colder the stones, and the ground is the coldest of all, and the bones of the dead are in the ground, but the dead are not cold, snow or no snow, it means very little to them, nothing, it means nothing to them, but for us, watching it snow on the dead, watching the graveyard get covered in snow, it is very cold, the snow on top of the graves over the bones, it seems especially cold, and at the same time especially peaceful, it is like snow falling gently on sleepers, even if it falls in a hurry it seems gentle, because the sleepers are gentle, they are not anxious, they are sleeping through the snow and they will be sleeping beyond the snow, and although I will be having sex while it snows I want to remember the quiet, cold, gentle sleepers who cannot think of themselves as birds nestled in feathers, but who are themselves, in part, part of the snow, which is falling with such steadfast devotion to the ground all the anxiety in the world seems gone, the world seems deep in a bed as I am deep in a bed, lost in the arms of my lover, yes, when it snows like this I feel the whole world has joined me in isolation and silence.

CAMP WILLIAM

This morning I want to talk a little bit about killing. You know it is never easy. There can never be enough killing. It is the biggest earthly part of time yet we are often shy of it. What a slow, discouraging business it can seem. It's fight, fight, fight and then some, with hardly a sign of encouragement to keep you going. But each of us must try. When we are young we are anxious to grow up and start killing but as soon as we are older we grasp the full measure of how difficult it really is. The secrets of the dark struggles of the night are well concealed. When I was a child my father often took me with him to visit various military installations, and to enter each one we had first to pass through a little gate where a guard waved at us and we were expected to wave back. It was of course really a salute, but really it looks something like a little wave, it *is* a little wave, and I was struck, as a child, by the fact two strangers — my father and the guard, who most certainly did not know each other — were expressing such open and friendly affection for each other. This wonderful feeling has never left me, and in many ways has led me to standing here before you today. If two strangers can express such unspoken goodwill toward each other, how much more so must take place when we are killing! For the greatest acts of killing take place between strangers, strangers for whom there exists this wonderful capacity for intimate connection. Think of it! Somewhere there exists a stranger waiting for you to kill him in such an honest and heartrending way. Or perhaps he will kill you, so glorious and inexplicable is life. I actually tremble when I speak of these things, for I know your hearts are good at the core, and that you are deserving of all life has to offer, and that one day your courage will burst its very vessels. Well, I will not keep you from your canoes any longer. But today when you are out rowing upon the waters, I hope each of you will take a moment to consider the strength you possess in your own two arms.

SUBURB OF LONG SUFFERING

Fire is my companion, but I do not talk to it, it talks to me. It has white-hot fissures that quiver and rage and complain and sometimes very tender speech towards morning, a low blue word or two. I never tire of listening to my fire. Music is my companion also, but it does not talk to me, I talk to it, I talk to it and it listens without complaint, absorbing whatever I am feeling and I can feel it listening to me. I think it never tires of listening to me. Together, the fire and the music and me, we make a family that, despite its dysfunction, is able to persevere. Yet I have a complaint. When they are in the room together, the fire and the music, they talk to each other and neither do they talk nor listen to me, as for example on a rainy day when the three of us come into the room together to while away the time: the fire and the music begin to converse in soft tones at first, so as not to disturb me I like to think, but soon their conversation grows to such a pitch that between the two of them there seem to be a great many unspoken agreements, while I am left feeling lonelier and lonelier, and end up by the window, a mere eavesdropper in my own home.

MY PET, MY CLOCK

A pet is a good way to tell time, better than a clock, for time is a measure of the changing positions of objects, and soon it will be time to feed the pet, to exercise the pet, to replace its little ball, clip its nails or talons, wash it ever so gently, vacuum up its sheddings and so forth. And eventually the sad day comes when it must die, and then it is time to get another. A clock, on the other hand and against all appearances, is a very poor way to tell time, for all it ever does is sit there or hang on the wall, and very seldom does it do anything of itself to remind you of time. Of course we live in a country where twice a year time springs forward or falls back, and on those occasions — the mock birthdays of time — a little fuss must be made over the clock, but other than that it does not really ask for much. If you are desirous of saving time one of the best things you can do is buy your clock batteries on one of its birthdays, eliminating the need for a gift on the next occasion. But other than these few inconveniences the care of your clock will never be a way of marking time, despite the fact we bring them into our homes for just this purpose. A clock is in fact no better than a dead pet. I myself have neither clock nor pet, and well might you ask what I do for time, though I prefer to put it somewhat differently: what has time ever done for me? Very little, it would seem; time has robbed me of my youth, my energy, strength, sprite, the vigor I was in my childhood famous for, and all the natural oils in my once-luxurious tresses. Once I felt enough for time to invest in a little goldfish, but alas he died two days later in a gallant attempt to jump his bowl, which was successful, though not in time, for in England there is a physicist by the name of Julian Barbour who believes time does not exist as we commonly perceive it to exist, that is in a passing continuum; no, he believes time, our time, time on earth, is made up of unconnected, absolutely discrete units, the length of an instant, which eternally occur, having no past and no future. In this sense of time, my goldfish is forever happily swimming in his new bowl and forever leaping from it in an adventurous frolic, or spasm of despair, depending on your view, which is also subject to time, as it is evident the views of old age do not coincide with youthful ones. But in this other world, the world of discrete eternal units, your pet needs his dinner, as he is whining at his bowl, yet does not need his dinner, as he has just eaten and is lying by the fire. Your pet has become a most inaccurate way of marking time, whereas the lifeless clock on the mantle, a discrete unit itself, dependent on no one and subject not to the passing of time, will finally have its day and serve its true purpose of marking time, which neither moves forward nor falls back, requiring no adjustments whatsoever, though, when this day comes and the clock is restored to its rightful place in our homes, if not our hearts, I often wonder if it will still be said when looking at a clock, as is the custom now, *how beautiful it is to have lived, how blessed that one can die.*

HAZELINE

After father died, he said that dying had taken a longer time than he had previously imagined possible. He was not dead at that time but we did not know it, his eyes had long ceased being the source of anything, he was stiff as a board and he had no pulse. Mother and I were very interested in everything he had to say, the way the living are with experts. He said it was extremely painful, even now, but not in any way that he could explain or describe. Speaking was painful, he said, more painful than anything else, because being dead — he couldn't describe it — it didn't amount to very much, there was no way we could understand, and by the time we ourselves died he would be long gone. He said there was a woman down the hall who was also dead, though no one knew it yet, and he could talk to her, but she wasn't listening. Mother bristled when he said this, and I put my hand on her arm. He was telling about how people when they are dead know each other by little signs that are not of this world when Doctor Fillmore came in and said Dad would be fine, though he didn't use those words exactly, he used "the old board with iron nails in it is an otter again." That was Dad. It didn't take anyone long to get to know him, a lot less time than it took to die, according to him who died six hours or days or weeks later, we could not be sure, as he had always been fond of making us feel we were floating away while he was standing on the coast of Iceland singing.

LICHEN

I wanted to go into the forest and collect lichen. I wanted to use the lichen in an art project because it had a crumbly, scaly texture and various shades of the same color appeared in the smallest patches. I was pretty sure lichen was rootless, but whether its living would be interrupted or unsettled in some way I was unsure. I didn't want to pick lichen if picking it in any way resembled kidnapping. I seemed to recall lichen was very old, among the oldest living things on earth, and that deserved considerable respect, but at the same time there had to be young lichen, if lichen was living it had to reproduce fairly regularly and so some of the lichen had to be young. I did not know how to tell young lichen from old lichen, I did not know if young lichen and old lichen lived together, I did not know which of them, the old or the young, was better suited to kidnapping, I thought it true in general that the older the living thing the closer it was to the end of its life cycle and the less harm there was in kidnapping it, but also true in general that the younger a thing, the less its grip was on its own life — in this case the rock or bark — and the more willing it would be to be lifted out of its environment, I mean the easier it would be to take. If the old lichen clung most tenaciously to its rock or bark, it would be more difficult to do the "right" thing, and if the young lichen could be fairly coaxed off the rock or bark, the easier it would be to do the "wrong" thing. I sat and had these thoughts before I put on my coat to go into the forest and collect my lichen. "My" lichen — it seemed already to be in my possession. To eliminate as much confusion as possible I decided I would collect only dead lichen. I knew that lichen was not of my species and certainly did not bury their dead; therefore the dead lichen must be everywhere in the forest, among the living, among the very old lichen and among the young lichen, and I would find them. But how? How could I recognize the dead lichen among the living lichen? Surely the dead lichen did not perceptively move, but nor did the living lichen perceptively move. I had to admit I could not tell the difference between the living and the dead. Such an incapacity shocked me. If that were my criteria it would be easier to collect bears, though, of course, in other ways, more difficult, and as I went out the door I understood, with some certainty I think, why bears are often on the minds of those who brave the forest.

A GLASS OF WATER

I needed to open the refrigerator — the water I wanted was there, sitting inside a glass pitcher on the uppermost grill, cold and clear and perfectly suited to my thirst. But I was afraid of the light, the light that went on whenever I opened the door, or the light that was always on — it was hard to tell — and I was more afraid of the light than I wanted the water. Still, my desire for the water was so strong I sometimes put my hand on the door, preparing, in my mind, to open the door more quickly than the light could respond to the door being opened, and sometimes I tried a completely spontaneous approach, believing if I opened the door *very* quickly, without thinking of either the water or the light, and most of all without thinking of opening the door (while I was opening it), I might be able to overcome the light, my fear, like most fear, being predicated on premeditation, but when this didn't work I entertained the very reasonable idea of waiting until the source of the light — the lightbulb — burned itself out, as was inevitable, though how this could happen if I didn't open the door once in all those years was a problem, compounded by the very real possibility of my dying of thirst while I waited. To use the light again and again seemed to be my only recourse if I wanted to burn the light out, and as it happened I opened the door again and again, but now I was more intent on the light than I was on the water, and forgot to drink altogether as I stood in the kitchen in my stocking feet in front of the refrigerator, opening and closing the door in rapid succession, driven by dehydration and fear to take risks that led me deeper and deeper into crisis.

WOMAN WITH A YELLOW SCARF

I was reading in bed in the morning, something I like to do, something I try to do every thirty days, two or three hours, usually on a Sunday. Reading in bed in the morning is not like reading at any other hour — first thing! — your mind fresh and alive and responsive, sometimes you read something you would miss at any other hour, especially the late ones, midnight, that's another time for reading and there are things you don't miss at midnight but they are not the things you don't miss in the morning. That was when I saw her. *A woman passed holding a yellow scarf over her head.* She does this in a story by Albert Camus. A French engineer is in a remote village in Brazil, the mayor has given him lodgings in the hospital, which is called by the curious name of "Happy Memory," which is not so curious when you consider the building of a hospital in a village that has none is a happy memory for those who live there and will use it. Our protagonist wakes up in Happy Memory hospital, it's raining, he looks out the window at a clump of aloes being rained on, and then the sentence happens. *A woman passed holding a yellow scarf over her head.* A simple sentence, of no import in the story — our lady never again appears, and without her presence on page 169 (in my copy) the story would not appear to be missing a single necessary moment. Yet the yellow scarf is needed by this woman at this moment, it is raining, she is passing by the hospital, she doesn't want to get her hair wet, or her head, or her body, luckily she has

26

a yellow scarf she can hold over her head, stretched like a sail between two hands, or maybe not, maybe the scarf is triangulated and she is holding it under her chin. Who is she? Where is she on her way to, or coming from, how old is she, is she married with children or not? What difference can it make, this fictional woman is born and dies in the same sentence, her moment passes us holding its yellow scarf, her fate is to appear in a story by Camus, and when I think of her fate I realize it could be worse, she could be walking past a window in a story by Thomas Gilbert, surely a woman can sense the importance of whose story she is in, perhaps that is why she chose, this morning, to bring along her yellow scarf — a keen author couldn't fail to notice that. Still, her fate cannot be commended, one day it is raining, she puts on a yellow scarf and goes out in the rain, never to be heard from or seen again. She is among the missing, but we don't even know her name, or what she looks like. I doubt the scarf was made of silk, canary yellow with a map of the world on it. I have such a scarf draped over a wooden hanger in my coat closet, I have had it many years and never once worn it, rain or no rain, I do not recall how I came by it, perhaps it was given to me. But in this remote village in Brazil in the nineteen hundred and fifties, this yellow scarf — well, maybe, ok, silk. I often fall into the habit of thinking anyone born in the ages before I was born lived in the dark ages. Nothing could be further from the truth, as they say, but I've noticed people everywhere stand as far from the truth as possible. *A woman passed holding a yellow scarf over her head.* I don't remember half the scarves or half the women

I see in an ordinary day. But this woman was different. She held her head up high as she walked across
the street in the rain, and I came to believe she was
on a mysterious and important errand, whose nature
I might never know, and that somewhere concealed
on her body she was carrying the tip of a forefinger
wrapped in a bit of yellow fur inside a white leather
ring box, and that the finger was mine, I had used it
to follow words, for words seemed to me to be always walking alone at night, even in broad daylight
they were walking alone at midnight, and I confess,
yes, I shadowed them, I shadowed them by way of
the alley that is always there and always empty and
narrow and hopeless and yields not a single clue.

THE BENCH

My husband and I were arguing about a bench we wanted to buy and put in part of our backyard, a part which is actually a meadow of sorts, a half- acre with tall grasses and weeds and the occasional wildflower because we do not mow it but leave it scrubby and unkempt. This bench would hardly ever be used and in the summer when the grasses were high would re- main partially hidden from view. We both knew we wanted the bench to be made of teak so that it would last a long time in the harsh weather and so that we would never have to paint it. Teak weathers to a soft silver that might, in November or March, disappear into the gray hills that are the backdrop of our lives. My husband wanted a four foot bench and I wanted a five foot bench. This is what we argued about. My husband insisted that a four foot bench was all we needed, since no more than two people (presumably ourselves) would ever sit on it at the same time. I felt his reasoning was not only beside the point but missed it entirely; I said what mattered most to me was the idea of the bench, the look of it there, to be gazed at with only the vaguest notion it could hold more people than would ever actually sit down. The life of the bench in my imagination was more im- portant than any practical function the bench might serve. After all, I argued, we wanted a bench so that we could look at it, so that we could imagine sitting on it, so that, unexpectedly, a bird might sit on it, or fallen leaves, or inches of snow, and the longer the bench, the greater the expanse of that plank, the more it matched its true function, which was imaginary. My husband mentioned money and I said that I was happier to have no bench at all, which would cost nothing, than to have a four foot bench, which would be expensive. I said that having no bench at all was closer to the five foot bench than the four foot bench because having no bench served the imagination in similar ways, and so not having a bench became an option in our argument, became a third bench. We grew very tired of discussing the three benches and for a day we rested from our argument. During this day I had many things to do and many of them involved my driving past other houses, none of which had benches, that is they each had the third bench, and as I drove past the other houses I could see a bench here and a bench there; sometimes I saw the bench very close to the house, against a wall or on a porch, and sometimes I saw the bench under a tree or in the open grass, cut or uncut, and once I saw the bench at the end of the driveway, blocking the road. Always it was a five foot bench that I saw, a long sleek bench or a broken-down bench, a bench with a slatted back or a bench with a solid, carved back, and always the bench was empty. But I knew that for my husband the third bench was only four feet long and he saw always two people sitting on it, two happy or tired people, two people who were happy to be alive or two people tired from having worked hard enough to buy the bench they were sitting on. Or they were happy and tired, happy to have reached the end of some argument, tired from having had it. For these people, the bench was an emblem of their days, which were fruitful because their suffering had come to an end. On my bench, which was always empty, nothing had come to an end because nothing had begun, no one had sat down, though the bench was always there waiting for exactly that to happen. And the bench was always long enough so that someone, if he desired to, could lie all the way down. That day passed. Another day followed it and my husband and I began, once more, to discuss the bench. The sound of our voices revealed a renewed interest and vigor. I thought I sensed in him a coming around to my view of the bench and I know he sensed in me a coming around to his view of the bench, because at one point I said that a four foot bench reminded me of rough notes towards a real bench while a five foot bench was like a fragment of an even longer bench and I admitted it was at times hard to tell the difference. He said he didn't know anything about the difference between rough notes and fragments but he agreed that between the two benches there was, possibly, just perhaps — he could imagine it — very little difference. It was, after all, only a foot we were talking about. And I think it was then, in both of our minds, that a fourth bench came into being, a bench that was only a foot long, a miniature bench, a bench we could build ourselves, though of course we did not. This seemed to be, essentially, the bench we were talking about. Much later, when the birds came back, or the leaves drifted downwards, or the snow fell, slowly and lightly at first, then heavier and faster, it was this bench that we both saw when we looked out the window at the bench we eventually placed in the meadow which continued to grow as if there were no bench at all.

MONUMENT

A small war had ended. Like all wars, it was terrible. Things which had stood in existence were now vanished. I had come back because I had survived and survivors come back, there is nothing else left for them to do. I had been on long travels connected to the war, and I had been to the centerpiece of the war, that acre of conflagration. And now I was sitting on a park bench, watching ducks land and take off from a pond. They too had survived, though I had no way of knowing if they were the same ducks from before the war or if they were the offspring of ducks who had died in the war. It was a warm day in the capital and people were walking without coats, dazed by the warmth, which was not the heat of war, which had engulfed them, but the warmth of expansion, in which would grow the idea of a memorial to the war, which had ended, and of which I was a veteran architect. I knew I would be called upon for my ideas in regards to this memorial and I had entered the park aimlessly, trying to escape my ideas, as I had been to the centerpiece, that acre of conflagration, and from there the only skill that returned was escapement, any others died with those who possessed them. I was dining with friends that evening, for the restaurants and theaters and shops had reopened, the capital was like a great tablecloth being shaken in mid-air so that life could be smoothed and reset and go on, and I had in my mind a longing to eat, and to afterwards order my favorite dessert, cherries jubilee, which would be made to flame and set in the center of the table, and I had in my mind the idea of submitting to the committee a drawing of an enormous plate of cherries, perpetually burning, to be set in the center of the park, as a memorial to the war, that acre of conflagration. And perhaps also in my mind was the hope that such a ridiculous idea would of course be ignored and as a result I would be left in peace, the one thing I desired, even beyond cherries. And I could see the committee, after abandoning my idea, remaining in their seats fighting over the designs of others, far into the after hours of the work day, their struggles never seeming to end, and then I wanted to submit an idea of themselves as a memorial for the war, the conference table on an island in the middle of the pond, though at least some of them would have to be willing to be cast in agony. And then I saw on the ground an unnamed insect in its solitary existence, making its laborious way through tough blades of grass that threatened its route, and using a stick that lay nearby I drew a circle around the animal — if you can call him that — and at once what had been but a moment of middling drama became a theater of conflict, for as the insect continued to fumble lop-sided in circles it seemed to me that his efforts had increased, not only by my interest in them, but by the addition of a perimeter which he now seemed intent on escaping. I looked up then, and what happened next I cannot describe without a considerable loss of words: I saw a drinking fountain. It had not suddenly appeared, it must have always been there, it must have been there as I walked past it and sat down on the bench, it must have been there yesterday, and during the war, and in the afternoons before the war. It was a plain gun-metal drinking fountain, of the old sort, a basin on a pedestal, and it stood there, an ordinary object that had become an unspeakable gift, a wonder of civilization, and I had an overwhelming desire to see if it worked, I stood up then and approached it timidly, as I would a woman, I bent low and put my hand on its handle and my mouth hovered over its spigot — I wanted to kiss it, I was going to kiss it — and I remembered with a horrible shock that in rising from the bench I had stepped on and killed the insect, I could hear again its death under my left foot, though this did not deter me from finishing my kiss, and as the water came forth with a low bubbling at first and finally an arch that reached my mouth, I began to devise a secret route out of the park that would keep me occupied for some time, then I looked up, holding the miraculous water in my mouth, and saw the ducks in mid-flight, their wings shedding water drops which returned to the pond, and remembered in amazement that I could swallow, and I did, then a bit of arcane knowledge returned to me from an idle moment of reading spent years ago, before the war: that a speculum is not only an instrument regarded by most with horror, as well as an ancient mirror, and a medieval compendium of all knowledge, but a patch of color on the lower wing segments of most ducks and some other birds. Thus I was able, in serenest peace, to make my way back to my garret and design the memorial which was not elected and never built, but remained for me an end to the war that had ended.

BEAUTIFUL DAY

I was walking to the post office when I happened to pass R——, a slight acquaintance on account of our having the same last name, as was discovered one year — oh, many years ago — at the voting poll. We were standing in line next to one another and I remember our conversation vividly. Actually we did not speak to one another, but when you are standing in line next to a man who precedes you into a narrow booth with a thick curtain hung on rings over a pole, and he is lost from view for a full five minutes which must be a terror for him as it will be for you, who can never remember the many names of the remarkable persons running for office, to the extent that on the previous evening I had written them in ballpoint on the palm of my hand, which was now sweating to the degree they had become illegible — well, as I insinuated, though we said nothing, how could we forget one another, thrown into circumstances like that? R—— came out of the booth, a volunteer called my name, and I think not a person in the room, which was overflowing with people, failed to note a person of one name preceded a person of the same name, or at the very least a person of one name following a person with the same name. Since our introduction then, almost nothing — an occasional nod, a nod of the head, yes, but a nod that is at once personal and touching, a charming, open, benevolent nod, this we sometimes exchanged, sometimes he initiated the nod and sometimes it was I, but I am a shy person, as is, I believe, constantly observed by those who live in this town. I was walking to the post office, I had walked all the way in fact and was now standing in front of it, when R—— said quite distinctly — I do not think I was imagining it — *hello*. I do not think a nod preceded this unexpected and curious addition to our relationship but I was shocked by its intimacy to the degree that I do not remember if a nod preceded it. Perhaps a nod came after? I cannot recall. Taking great care not to lose control over my faculties altogether I said to R——: *hello*. This word, following so soon after the first, stunned me with the power of communication possible between two souls who have heretofore labored so intently to keep their human capacity for passion latent. At that moment I realized it was a beautiful day — indeed it was a very beautiful day, overabundant, radiant in all aspects of itself, the flag flying like a certificate of rapturous appreciation for the clouds, which were sailing directly overhead across a clear blue sky, and in the window boxes attached to the brick façade of the building pert crocuses stood in a bright array, it seemed to me they were like responsive ears, alert to whatever R—— or I might venture to say next; perhaps it was on account of this fantasy that I hesitated, I hesitated to speak what I felt and say what I knew to be true: *it is a beautiful day*. But would such a confession, I asked myself in my hesitation, be too prompt, too rash, coming so soon after the two *hellos*, which had already fallen in such rapid progression that R—— might, like myself, be quaking from an inability to keep up with all that had already happened? Might R—— feel I was pushing the day forward at an alarming and unjust rate, even if part of its undeniable beauty was that very quickening? These thoughts and more like them prevented the spontaneous expression I should have liked so much to make before R—— was gone. R—— did not hesitate, that is for certain — he sailed like a cloud into the post office, nod or no nod (why wasn't I paying *more attention?*) and I was stuck fast by the crocuses, the flag unfurled over us all, when the decision came over me to begin my way home, immediately and with brio, that I might lose no further step with the day, which was beautiful, and with the future which had shown itself to be quick but kind, allowing me these little moments to catch up with it, and keep pace with it when I could.

MY SEARCH AMONG THE BIRDS

Aug 19 It took the little birds — are they wrens? — about a week to find the seeds.

Aug 23 One day a pigeon joined them, he was larger and seemed "superior," the wrens seemed "respectful," as if they were deferring to him.

(later) I saw a bird in the bushes near Dairy Queen. It looked thin to me.

(later) There were about ten little wrens at work on the seed when someone on the street revved up a motorcycle — nine of the wrens instantly flew to the nearest tree, all together, but one little wren did not — he just stayed and kept on eating.
a) was he smarter than the others?
b) was he dumber than the others?
c) was he simply deaf?

A minute later all the wrens in the tree flew off together and when the wren who stayed behind to work on the seed *saw* them (with his eyes) he instantly joined them — he didn't want to be left behind! But when they were just going to the tree he hadn't minded one bit.

Aug 24 A hawk circling very high up in the heavens.

Aug 25 Some of the birds have told me their names; the rest are so far quiet.

(later) I dare not log the amount of time I spend sitting on the ledge of the kitchen window, watching the wrens on the flat black asphalt roof where I have placed a red frisbee of water and a blue frisbee of seed.

Aug 26 They come for breakfast and they come for dinner. WHERE DO THEY GO FOR LUNCH?

Aug 28 Bought a pair of opera glasses to facilitate my search among the birds.

Aug 29 I replace the little golden seeds, for I have run out of them, with black oiled sunflower seeds, which everyone knows are superior and preferred by all birds. I do this in the middle of the night so as to "surprise" the birds in the morning. But in the morning they don't act "surprised" at all, they act as if nothing's changed. But then again, they may be "acting."

(later) They ARE acting — the wrens don't like the new seed, they are ignoring it! Do they KNOW how much work it took to lug that bag up the stairs?

Aug 30 Now the pigeon comes around and does a terrible thing, an inexplicable thing — he scatters all the seed by standing in the frisbee and with his head down in the seed swings his head from side to side, not eating but *sweeping* the seeds out of the frisbee and onto the roof, all over the roof; he seems angry, as if he's searching for something he can't find.

(later) The truth is, none of us really feed the birds because we care for them; we feed them because we like to watch.

(later) But was the PIGEON caring for the birds? Was the big bird caring for the little birds? Because now that the big seeds are SCATTERED, all the little wrens come and eat them joyfully off the roof.

Sept 1 Early this morning a cardinal appears out of nowhere, looking like Santa Claus.

(later) Suddenly it occurs to me this just might be the birds' Christmas — I must do something quick, something special.

(later) Went out and bought six paper bags of French fries, carefully arranging them in the frisbee so their ends were up.

(later) A dove comes, a pale gray soft dove, smaller than the pigeons but larger than the wrens. Doves are lovebirds, how can they come in anything less than a pair? My medium dove must be a heartbroken one.

My French fries are eaten by the medium heartbroken dove.

Is there anything sadder than the sight of a medium heartbroken dove stuffed with French fries on Christmas morning?

Sept 2 Is there anything better, more beautiful, in all the world, across all the lands, over the Taj Mahal and everything, than two pigeons, ten wrens, a cardinal, and a medium heartbroken dove come to Ohio, to an asphalt roof, to eat potatoes on the day AFTER Christmas?

(later) A piece of available sky.

Sept 3 Wrens are described as having "upturned tail feathers," that being their DISTINGUISHING feature, and my little browny-gray birds do NOT — mine have flat, outgoing tails like musical reeds.

(later) Is it that we can never name that which we love?

Sept 4 I would look it up in a book, but it is a sin to look up that which you love in a book.

Sept 9 Most beautiful blackbird I've ever seen — sleek, all sheen, positively indigo head/throat, wearing a turquoise necklace on top of that!

Sept 10 Susan says the little wren-who-is-not-a-wren, the one who stayed to gorge while the others fled, was displaying "desperate gluttony," a condition in which he repressed his deeper, more constant, tragic terror, out of which arose indomitable seed greediness, a mere symptom of deeper hungers. I think this means he stayed because he was MORE terrified than the others, not less.

Sept 11 One pigeon (rock dove!) is magnificently all brown in the body, but his tail is white. He looks like a horse.

Sept 12 On December 9, 1531, the Indian neophyte Juan Diego was lured to Mount Tepeyac by the sound of stunning music. He made his way to the top and the Virgin of Guadalupe appeared to him in radiant splendor. Could it have been a thrush?

Sept 13 This morning all the little gray-brown no-names looked fuzzier than usual — I thought they were baby chicks toddling in a barnyard.

Sept 14 The Bible says we are living through the greatest mass-extinction period in the planet's history.

Sept 15 When I buy my weekly bag of seeds at Ace Hardware, a 25-lb bag for eight dollars and some cents, the man I buy them from carries the bag out to my car for me, and I thank him. This doesn't seem worth noting, except whenever it happens I have the distinct impression we are being watched.

Sept 17 I don't know what has happened, but all my little gray-browns have disappeared and a similar number of VERY PLUMP gray-browns have taken their place! Lined up on the telephone wire — which overhangs the roof — they look like a bunch of beer bottles, or a line of tits, which is the same thing.

Sept 18 Although all poets aspire to be birds, no bird aspires to be a poet.

Sept 19 If I don't feed them for a single day, they stop coming! And I look back over my life, to an autumn day years and years ago, when my (then) therapist told me there are very few things one can take personally; apparently I am still struggling with this.

Sept 20 Some days just to tell a bird from a tree is asking a lot.

Sept 21 Though this country was founded on principles of freedom, nowhere in the United States Constitution do they mention birds.

Sept 22 Kate and Pete keep frozen yellow finches in their freezer, in zip-lock bags, for the purposes of "drawing and photography."

Sept 23 I lost my long brown wallet, and in it were my credit card, my debit card, my checkbook, my checkbook register, my video club card, my Osco card, my Grand Union card, my Co-op card, my oil-change card, my automobile club card, my driver's license, my medical insurance card, my cash, my change, my slips and bits of paper with the names of books, films, and musical recordings I want to experience before I die, the names and numbers of human beings I could call if I were ever in an emergency or lost or sad, and when I lost my long brown wallet with all this stuff in it, I felt like a bird, and it was wonderful.

Sept 24 Eating dinner on the window ledge, I am watching my birds as I gnaw on a chicken thigh.

There I am, chewing my dead bird in front of living birds. As soon as I realize this, I am ashamed, and keep on eating.

Sept 25 What if half the people you knew, and half the people you loved, were dead within a year? Last night on the phone Ralph was so depressed I didn't know what to do, so I said, out of the blue, "Do you want to talk about the avian flu?"

(later) Sorrow thy name is sparrow.

Sept 27 With folded wings.

Sept 28 No more prayers. Say instead, as many times as you can, the word SPARROW. Soon you will be saying O SPARE O SPARE O SPARE O SPARE.

Sept 29 In the palm of the child's hand is a bird.

(later) The Gypsies have a name for it.

THE DART AND THE DRILL

I do not believe that when my brother pierced my skull with a succession of darts thrown from across our paneled rec room on the night of November 18th in my sixth year on earth, he was trying to transcend the notions of time and space as contained and protected by the human skull. But who can fathom the complexities of the human brain? Ten years later — this would have been in 1967 — *The New York Times* reported a twenty-four-year-old man, who held an honor degree in law, died in the process of using a dentist's drill on his own skull, positioned an inch above his right ear, in an attempt to prove that time and space could be conquered. He had taken a tab of acid an hour earlier and, in a state of expanded — some might say exaggerated — consciousness, hit upon this singular proof. Ever since my brother darted me I have lived in a state of expanding consciousness — mine grew and grew until they called me old — but not once have I taken a drill to myself. I have considered a gun. I have worn hats. I have had a magnificent hairdresser. The art of trepanning — surgically cutting out discs of bone from the skull using a trephine — derives from the art of mining rock by using a similar tool for sinking shafts; who has not wondered what it would be like to journey to the center of the earth, and who has not coveted what valuables can be picked up on the way down? Necklaces and bracelets and rings bear witness to our desire to imitate the young man and his conquering drill — to seek, to mine, to plunder, to uncover what is buried deep beneath some surface. My mother always wore a gold linked bracelet because it was given to her by a boy she fancied before she met my father. This boy wanted to know my mother, but how far he got in their ice-cream soda conversations is not known to me, it being safe to say my father got further in *his* late-night conversations, trepanning her mind with a nonchalance and skill I can only imagine, trepanning her mind for another fifty years, at which point he gave her his own gold tooth hanging from a chain, about which she had very little to say, and said it by never wearing it. The human brain seems to be obsessed with boring into other brains, and if none are available, one's own brain will do quite well, if one is smart enough to see that mysteries lie within as well as without, and you would be surprised, actually, to know how few are left on earth who seriously consider themselves worth investigating, and, sadly, our young man with a drill is no longer among them. Astronauts and mechanical rovers always dig a little when they reach another planet, while there is a shaft in the desert here that never stops hauling, and certain mines have been in continuous operation for centuries. Across time, across space, the ruby and emerald-throated hummingbirds fly, with their exquisitely long beaks working nonstop to dart the flowers. There is that, O my brother, and in the summer of love one young human, high on life itself, plugged in an electric drill to see what he would find. What is more, regardless of how he tried to settle these matters, no one has ever stopped trying, no one has ever stopped and said *Enough*, all these things do is make us shudder.

THE TAKING OF MOUNDVILLE BY ZOOM

If you were very, very small, smaller than a lepre-chaun, smaller than a gnome or a fairy, and you lived in a vagina, every time a penis came in there would be a natural disaster. Your dishes would fall out of the cupboards and break and the furniture slide all the way to the other side of the room. It would take a long time to clean up afterwards.

HARD-BOILED DETECTIVE

If you believe what you have been told, men and women have sex and sex leads to pregnancy and pregnancy produces every known person on the planet. But you have to look beneath the surface. You have to ask questions. How many pregnant women do you actually know? How many pregnant women have you known in your lifetime? If you have known more than twenty you are truly extraordinary. Let's say you are extraordinary. You are a gynecologist! You see twenty pregnant women a day! But you see the same twenty pregnant women a day for nine months. There are twelve months in a year. Even if you worked for fifty years, you would only see one thousand pregnant women, and there are *seven billion* people in the world. In any one of the world's teeming cities, today, at this hour, there are millions of people threading in and out of the shops, in offices, ordering from menus. There are people alone in their rooms, dozing, watering plants, talking on telephones. Did you picture any of these people as pregnant? Of course not, because so few actually are. How many times have you yourself been pregnant? Not seven billion times! Granted, if each person on the planet was pregnant only once, that would account for everyone. But that never happens, it can't happen, it's impossible, there are children, there are the elderly, the infertile, the young girls on birth control, the abortions. I live in a town of 20,000 people and only two were born today. I am conducting my investigations at three o'clock in the afternoon, and it is possible many of my town's inhabitants are having sex at this moment, but it is impossible that they are in the majority. Even at midnight, it's a hard case to crack, because although more people are actually having sex at that hour, in today's world not half the sex we are having actually leads to pregnancy. It doesn't add up. You do the math. In summation: How many pregnant women do you actually know? How may pregnant women did you see on the street today? Now look at all the people in the world. Where did they come from? A deep mystery remains unsolved. Perhaps I go too far, but I think it is the fundamental mystery of life.

WHAT WOMAN

If someone asked me to remember my first menses — for what woman can forget it? — I would remember the afternoon in the dressing room off of the ballet studio, where I was one of twelve disciples in pink and black who had just been whipped to a frenzy in front of a mirror by a Russian voice, and the low bench where I sat undoing my toe shoes, unwinding their long ribbons from around my ankles, mysteriously feeling that my unseen toes had been crushed in a new way, a way that ushered in the idea that love could be greater than pain, devotion could withstand the greatest barbarity, and I was one who could bear it. That wad of lamb's wool stuffed in the blunt end of each shoe was indeed blood-soaked, it was wet, it was red, and yet already turning a dark and troubling purple.

ALL MY ROE

The mystery of mysteries was not a thing to be spoken lightly of, night after night we guessed but never asked, it meant that we were on our way to the Earth, a convulsive shudder now and then and one of us would leave, it was the end of slumber, there would be object lessons, butter, sugar, cake and bones, but never the times we talked late into the fire and adored one another the way we were just there, just together, we would never speak of it but it was there, and never again a comrade like that, to open a door and find everything in love, which somehow made us, daylight we never looked at and went by with a run, out of that door we believed came time, we guessed but never asked, possible back after away and over again we did not know, there was never a weeping like ours, a thousand good nights so next to the next we did not have to speak, who we are we don't know, we are heard thoughts we think, there is a mystery in our atmosphere as yet of nothing and I, the uninitiated, the untried, venture to ask the little beggars of the old Earth each to say a word about it, I did every now and then watch some of them come to the edge of a wide water, and pause, one foot in the air, looking with their keen eyes across it, and swim over, one after the other, till they were all out of sight, and I could only guess where they were by the screaming birds above them.

PEEK-A-MOOSE

And I knew somewhere deeply recessed, "away from it all," the real with-it-all took place; there, in the undulating mists, a moose eating the dark green mosses was barely seen through the pines, which were repossessed in the animal's eyebrows (do moose have eyebrows?), craggy and overhanging like the mist and the moss, and all around him millions upon millions of other moose lie dead and buried, and no one had ever had a peek of them (though there were glimpses), and in the glare light of the pizza parlor I chose anchovies which I did not like but seemed ancient and suffering, such small animals, and I took the pie home with me and ate it with my mouth gaping, painfully aware I was not a moose and had never been a moose and would never be a moose, but I had loved you in such an eerie and unnatural way.

SLEEP

She wakes in the middle of the night and puts on a robe, goes to the tap, draws a glass of water, stands at the window, and we can speculate she knows she is not the only person on the planet but at this moment she, our insomniac, believes the others, most of the others in this world, are all peacefully sleeping, which is an illusion, it is not night everywhere, just as in daylight she believes in an endless sky, an illusion, outside the sixty-two vertical miles of pale air — an hour's drive — it is in fact night everywhere and at all times, night is night is night out *there*, but that is just another illusion, night depends on day, no day no night, there is no night there then but something else, something dark and endlessly there in a nightish way. Beyond this, what do we know about our insomniac really? We do not know what her thoughts are but we know she is having them because the expression on her face tells us there is a lot going on inside her head, just as we know from the face of a sleeper that he is dreaming, though we know not what his dreams are. And then — it is now three a.m. — someone wakes in Chicago, someone wakes in Omaha, someone wakes in Denver, and in Minneapolis someone wakes, the robe, the tap, the water, the window, the beliefs, the illusions, the faces, the unknown thoughts. She looks out the window at the snow falling gently in the parking lot, falling on the parked cars and the metal dumpster, the street lights are on and illuminate whole shafts of gently falling snow and there is a lone rabbit out

there, hopping and then stopping, hopping and stopping in the snow under the light in the middle of the
night, this rabbit, out in the world and disappearing
into its shadows.

A CERTAIN SWIRL

The classroom was dark, all the desks were empty, and the sentence on the board was frightened to find itself alone. The sentence wanted someone to read it, the sentence thought it was a fine sentence, a noble, thorough sentence, perhaps a sentence of some importance, made of chalk dust, yes, but a sentence that contained within itself a certain swirl not unlike the nebulous heart of the unknown universe, but if no one read it, how could it be sure? Perhaps it was a dull sentence and that was why everyone had left the room and turned out the lights. Night came, and the moon with it. The sentence sat on the board and shone. It was beautiful to look at, but no one read it.

ASCRIBED THIS DAY TO THE AFFIDAVIT

The street cleaner woke us at five a.m.; from those first distant sounds we were awestruck, and when we looked out it seemed the most beautiful apparition in the world. It was big as a parade float and moved just as slowly, a strange glowing thing whose whir-ring was now upon us. We tiptoed out to the street and commenced to follow it. One of us had the idea to sprinkle cinnamon in its wake and, all being in general agreement, this is what we did. We followed the truck as it made its ablutionary rounds washing the asphalt with those stiff and rotating brushes, while we shuffled and stooped behind, sprinkling the spice. Thus we completed our dawn devotion, and the world was fragrant and clean, though, to the best of our knowledge, none of the sleepers, when they awoke, were aware of the act that had taken place in the dark, and on their behalf.

THE DIARY

My father was a diary farmer and I grew up on a diary farm. Though it was a small farm, tucked in a valley of rolling pasture bordered by high forest, we always had at least a hundred diaries, four journals and a small cache of notebooks for our own personal use. My job, as far back as I can remember, was to look forward to being happy. In the morning before the mist lifted off, before I walked down the dirt road a good three miles to where it joined the paved road that led to the schoolhouse, it was my job to go into the barn and read the diaries. I could only read one or two at most, before setting off for school, but my father was thankful for even that small amount of hope, and my mother never complained so long as my homework was done. I would sit in the straw on the barn floor, the earliest light streaming in through cracks in the wall, like the shaft of light the movie projector made in the darkened town hall on Friday nights, and some of the chaff from the barn floor floating in that light, particles of straw we used to cover the diaries and other stuff, all afloat in a never-ending stream of hope as I lay on the floor and read. We gave all our diaries personal names, and though most people think diaries are all alike, my experience of watching them grow from a mere sentence to a full-blown lock-and-key affair taught me that no two diaries are alike and, like us, each diary deserves its own name. There were general traits, yes; it's true that all diaries prefer stillness to commotion, and for the most part are happiest in the shade and not the sun, but it is equally true that some diaries possess a need to be around other diaries, while some like to be by themselves, and some like to be talked to constantly, while others wander off if you so much as say a word. You'd be surprised by Bessie, a diary I raised from birth, who did her best work wearing a scarf. That was Bessie, who was completely unmanageable until the morning I untied my long woolen scarf and wrapped her in it. When my mother, an otherwise long-suffering and compliant woman, heard I had gone to school without my scarf, she went into the barn to try and take the scarf from Bessie; she did not succeed — mother never did identify with the diaries the way I did — but that night bit her lip in front of me and was forever after that after me for my spelling. I think it was not long afterwards the herd began to thin. Small farmers like my father couldn't compete with the commercial franchises that were subsidized by the government in exchange for meeting a homogenized standard of production. I was in high school by then, and watched my father go from a lean, happy man, proud to be a farmer, to an old, disturbed man, oiling his shotgun in the shed. The herd *had* thinned. Gone were the days we delivered door to door. Gone were the journals we actually read (eventually we were reduced to renting our journals each spring to the commercial men who released them among their own diaries in an effort to improve their heads). The notebooks that we had helped birth on our hands and knees, the notebooks that the family raised so that every Easter they could be opened and read aloud at our own planked table, these resisted the changing times as long as they could, but the day came — I was home from college — my father announced we were going into town to buy a notebook, as our last one had died and it wasn't cost-effective to raise even a sentence from scratch. That was a sad meal, our last before mother passed and father had to lease the acreage to the Salisbury crew. And then — and then — at the very end, at the moment our plan was to sell the farm and move father to a home in town where they had books, at the very moment we were reduced to two diaries and a dog, and not a single notebook or journal still belonged to us, two miracles happened. The first was a fast-developing grass roots movement dedicated to the old diary ways, and a group came forward willing to buy our two remaining diaries for a hefty sum. The second was an explosive market for diary run-off — that would be ash — which had been proved to contain enough potassium to feed a city the size of Kansas. Ash was one thing we had plenty of, for the ashes of old diaries, of pages and ribbons and bindings and backs, had been piling up in the nooks and crannies of our dilapidated barn since before I was born. We had enough genuine ash on the farm to feed the nation. And it was then that my father took a renewed interest in the lives of others, and left the farm to me, and it was I who installed the sifting machines, and I who lived to see the ashes of a lifetime rise again in the barn; night and day they rose, and I could always find a moment or two to myself, especially after father passed, a moment when the chaff-filled beams of light brought back those golden afternoons of my youth, when my job was to look forward to being happy, and here I was, all those years later, in the barn, remembering the old days when a diary would get sick and one of us would have to sit up with it all night long, huddled under the blankets and using a flashlight to keep it calm.

THE MOST OF IT

My Aunt Miel, who never married and whom I never met, was eccentric, and the most of it was her handwriting. She was my mother's sister, and lived at a distance, having gotten a job with the Singer Sewing Machine Company which required her to sit in a storefront and sew so everyone could see for themselves each marvelous new electric model. Everyone said she was made for the job, as she was small of stature and tireless. When she wasn't sewing dresses in the window, her gleaming machine the envy of every woman who walked by, and herself, my mother once told me, the envy of every man who walked by, she wrote us long letters, and their arrival on Thursdays attracted neighborhood attention. Aunt Miel's handwriting was so large no one could read it — at least not easily, or in the usual way. My mother had to stand on our tenement roof to read Aunt Miel's letter, which my sister and I would carefully unfold on the street below. When I was six, one of my favorite games was to stand inside of the Os, and then lie down, for they encircled me perfectly from head to toe, and though there was no point to the game, I would wander happily from O to O, sometimes hopping when there were two in a row, as in the word *soon*. My sister preferred the Ts, on top of which she would align herself with her arms spread out and lie there batting her eyelashes at my mother above. Whenever the word *Tom* occurred, my sister and I would lie on our letters side by side, and her hand would be touching my head. Procuring paper had always been a problem for Aunt Miel, especially during the Depression, but as she had a job she was able, whenever she went to the butcher's (my mother said, too, that Miel was famous for her minced pork) to buy whole rolls of his meat-wrapping paper, which she would unroll into longer and longer sheets, then cut with a pair of Singer sewing scissors, pasting together as many sheets as she needed to say what she had to say. It seemed she was incapable of anything less. My mother said when Miel was a little girl, and indeed she never grew up to be very big, Miel and her handwriting were the scourge of the household; from the time she first learned her letters they were gargantuan. On her very first day of school she sat at her desk with tears in her eyes, staring down at the little piece of paper in front of her, unable to use it. Her teacher, who was kind, gave her a stub of chalk and allowed Miel to write on the blackboard, but in a week or two, as soon as Miel went over the edge, the kindness stopped and Miel was punished with a ruler and then a yardstick, and then the dreaded paddling began. But the day she began to write on the ground nothing could stop her, they had to let a thing like that go. Soon the hallway floors of her school were covered with Miel's little exercises, which stayed there just long enough for her teachers to read them, correct them, grade them and call for the janitor to come mop them up. By the time she earned her certificate, the letters had stopped growing and were the same size as the ones I saw as a child, when I would lie down inside of her Os like a baby. Sadly, her letters were too long to keep, sometimes twenty-five feet or longer, and after an hour or two, before the men came home and the street was needed for their passing, my mother and her friends would tear Aunt Miel's letters along the lines of the original sheets she had pasted together, and every woman would take an armload home to burn in her stove. But the Thursdays they came were wonderful days, days I shall never forget, with my mother up on our roof, and all of the women in the neighborhood alerted by her standing there that a letter had come, and then the communal reading would begin, and it was a sight, what with the skirts and dresses and aprons billowing out on the roofs and fire escapes and balconies, and all of the heads hanging out of the windows, and Aunt Miel's life utterly exposed to the world, while the children below couldn't care a jot, and were happy and safe and warm, just finding a letter they could crawl into and call their own.

A ROMANTIC POET AND HIS DESTINY

Born into a family, H enjoyed an abundance of comforts and was provided a sound education, thanks to his uncle. Upon entering the world of commerce, H did not like banking, he did not like retailing, and he did not like practicing the law. What H liked were daughters. They liked H too, but not as much as they liked the phrase *auf wiedersehen*. Failure and rejection fertilized H. He wandered here and there, across hills and through valleys, composing songs. As time passed, little H became big. People tried to find him. He gravitated toward fountains and promoted their fallen charms. This shift in his writing style did not really change the world. Secret French money kept him alive — albeit he was surrounded by German spies. Living a tricky life was tiresome, so every seven months for seven years he cleared the skies with an illiterate girl. She convinced him to turn forty-four, but sadly he was confined to bed thereafter, by what the Germans call the French malady and the French call the German disease. He married the dear girl, often eating crackers in bed and writing on napkins. After he died, his whole estate went to his widow on the condition she would marry again so there would be at least one man to regret his passing.

IF ALL THE WORLD WERE PAPER

If you bother to read this at all it is a clear indication your life is intolerable and you seek a distraction by engaging in the activity you are presently pretending to engage in. I say *pretending* because you would never have reached the conclusion your life is intolerable had you not also reached the conclusion it is unreal. But long before one of the living comes to such a conclusion — that life is unreal — he first passes through the conclusion that reading is unreal, unreal because it is literally an imaginative act, so much so that no one *actually* reads, and has not *actually* read since they first learned how, compounded, of course, by the present-day fact no one "actually" reads anymore anyway. But little do any of your problems bother me on such a fine day! And it *is* a fine day, a fine day in plain view to anyone who happens to look up from their reading. All day I look at the grass. A woman in a big hat walks by. I sneeze. Occasionally I feel I am being born. At such moments of birth I am seized by a feeling of frightening abundance. There are too many trees in the world. There are too many trees and too many people, far too many people; there is too much shampoo and too much toothpaste, too much pollution, dirt, rocks and grass — far too much grass. The birds — too many of them fly. Don't bother counting, you'll never come to an end. Ditto pencils and pens. Don't mention books! Have you come to the part where I am only pretending to write? Surely you can tell I am only pretending to write. This is what pretending to write looks like, it looks like this. Not a landscape and yet passing before your eyes, unrolling as featureless as a plain and often you are the antelope, scared to have been born under such dismal skies. And you, aren't you only pretending to read? Yes, I can feel it, I can feel your eyes on my back, and I grant you, antelope, I am afraid, and the only way I can control my fear — of you pretending to read — is to go on pretending to write, and so long as I go on, you too shall go on. Isn't existence grand, the grandest bond between two you can imagine? Doesn't it outstrip your finest memory? Memories are worthless, have you ever stopped to consider that? Do you remember being by the seashore and watching the great broom of the sea come sweeping down on the shore, pushing all the glinty particles of sand out of its way? The sound of the sea's broom was so tremendous it sloshed the fluid in your ears. What did you come to the beach for anyway? Summer reading? What a pretense! Reading can't slosh the fluid in your ears the way a wave can. And the equatorial grass of the dunes looks and grows as a woman's hair when it is long and dry and white as parsnips. Parsnips, cut into disks and sautéed with an onion and a little garlic in a green pool of olive oil, could fool anyone into thinking they were something finer, nobler, more expensive and rare, not unlike the experience of dining on a well-prepared rabbit. The rabbit, another exquisite subject one could write a book about! One wonders, for example, whether there are more rabbits in the world than books, or more books than rabbits. Either way, what has happened to the world since its inception is condensed in the specimen of a single hare. It is real and it has reproduced itself, eaten parsnips and grasses, and been condemned to die at a railroad crossing. Soon the trains, too, shall pass out of all being, while books, I'm afraid, will go on pretending they are still among us. My friend — for nothing hinders me from calling you my friend, especially the fact we have never met, and are only now pretending to — if all the world were made of paper, and perhaps it is, it could one day conceivably burn for years, like the rainforests of Brazil were once so fond of doing, and eventually we'd be reduced to a few square heaps of ash, as if the sun had strayed too close, or one among us drifted too far, the sensitivity of his organs of perception so extreme he regarded all of civilization, and most of literature, an illusion.

A MINOR PERSONAL MATTER

For a long time I was a poet. That is, I used to be a poet, for quite a long time in fact, and made my life making poems and teaching persons younger than myself just what this entailed, although I myself had no idea what it entailed, beyond a certain amount of courage and a certain amount of fear, but these amounts were variable and it was not always possible to say in which order they appeared and at any rate it was hard to convey. It was harder and harder to convey, but conveying it became easier and easier and that, too, lent an air of confusion to my days. For instance, many days I did not care about saying any of this, I only cared to say certain things that might cause someone to like me, but of course I never said that. I said only that I cared to say certain things that might cause someone to like the language. This seemed foolish because whether or not someone liked the language they had no choice but to use it. Whether or not the language was beautiful or gruff or strange they had no choice but to use it. So I said I only cared to say certain things that might cause someone to like the world, and being alive in it. This seemed foolish because whether or not someone liked the world they had no choice but to live in it. Whether the world was beautiful or gruff or strange they had no choice but to live. Yes, I said, you may kill yourself, but that would not be living, you would not be living then. A great many poets killed themselves. This was a problem too insurmountable to even understand, although at times I felt I understood it very closely and this also was part of the problem. The only thing that seemed certain to me was that people who had no choice but to use the language while they were alive had a choice in whether or not they liked me. This was a real choice, one I might be able to persuade them in. And so it seemed to me this reason, the one which sounded most foolish of all (and therefore I never spoke it) was actually the most reasonable of all. Still, occasionally I met people who did not seem to like me no matter what I said or did. And it was not easy to turn away from them because they were the challenge. They were the challenge because they challenged me to like myself even if they did not. That was the challenge — to like myself in spite of all that happened or did not happen to me. It was to face this challenge that I ceased to write poems. Could I like myself if I no longer engaged in an activity I openly declared was the reason I was put on the planet in the first place? Would I find another reason to be on the planet, or could I remain on the planet, with nothing to do and no one to like me, liking myself? I decided to try. I was on the planet with nothing to do and no one to like me. And as soon as I found myself there, I realized I had created the circumstances in which I had begun to write poems in the first place, to the extent I now wander the earth, a ghost, with no intent to write, but carrying a spark in my fingertips, which keeps me in a state of constant fibrillation, neither dead nor alive, a will-o'-the-wisp of stress, art, and the hours.

ON TWILIGHT

I read the poem of a student and in the poem God wandered through a room picking up random objects — a pear, a vase, a shoe — and in bewilderment said, "I made this?". Apparently God had forgotten making anything at all. I awarded this poem a prize, because I was a judge of such matters. I was not really awarding the student, I was awarding God; I knew someday the student would pick up his old poem and say in bewilderment, "I made this?", and at that moment his whole world would be lost in the twilight, and when you are finally lost in the twilight, you cannot judge anything.

UNIVERSITY OF THE LIMITLESS MOUSE

The University of the Limitless Mouse was more or less like any other university, except for exams: students sat for suet every four months, eating a block of it, spitting the seeds into little cups passed out for that purpose, and were given a bar of motel soap for washing their hands afterwards. Those unfortunates who swallowed the seeds grew into huge and solitary trees whose sole purpose was to shade the campus from anything that might come to it from above. The provost liked particularly the roots of these trees and saw to it they were strong. The day did come however when *the old pumpkin fricasseed in snow* (as he liked to call himself in a show of learning) died, and not long afterward the academy closed out of respect for the melancholy. The tree roots, which had risen above ground like enormous braids of bread dough, shrank back to withered veins. The limitless supply of mice, no longer instructed or even able to lose themselves in the great maze of roots, stretched to the horizon, and it was here, among them, I now wandered, one to whom it had always been curious that the failed, the seed-swallowers, should have been so favored, though none of the other mice shared my curiosity, and indeed, on the point of starving, they now began to devour the entire system of roots down to six million pounds of what, in the final stages of that learned feast, looked like ash. And so it was that I alone passed down the road of questioning, which was deserted and giving out black smoke from those broken individuals, about whom so little is known and so much has been written.

SOME NONDESCRIPT AUTUMN WEEKEND

Remove everything beautiful from your home, remove everything you like, love, cherish or are fond of. Remember to include pets and people. Remove everything which reminds you of these things in any way. Remove everything which brings you happiness or a feeling of peace. Remove everything which reminds you of your life.

Leave everything which you feel is ugly, disgusting, broken or painful. Leave everything that makes you uncomfortable when you look at it or use it. If necessary, add to these things by bringing more of them from the outside in. Make sure your home is as full as it once was and be certain everything is crummy and repulsive. Live in this space, among these things you cannot bear, for sixty days.

Empty the space completely. Leave nothing in it. Clean it thoroughly and wash the windows. Sleep on the floor, or on a clean thin mattress the exact dimensions of your own body. Live in this space for sixty days, during which your primary activity, when you are home, is to stare at the ceiling.

Bring the beautiful things back in, bring your beloved belongings, your most cherished possessions, back into the space and place them in their original positions. Make sure everything is as it was before. Live as you once did; if this is not possible, live twice.

A HALF-SKETCHED HEAD

THIS IS WHY

It was of no use, trying to discern whether the anchorite was happy or unhappy; in the first days of her visit Mary assumed this was why she had come, but the longer she stayed the more she felt at home, the more she felt at home, the more she felt free to be miserable, and finally Mary saw that the question was useless.

REGRETS

The anchorite was in the habit of keeping lists. Among them Mary noticed a continuing list of regrets, under that heading, and though many of them were crossed off or blackened out, new ones were added as well. Mary asked him if a kind of balance were kept, to which he replied: "If only! As a matter of fact, your question is an item I have been tempted to add to the list."

CHILDHOOD MEMORIES

There was a long silence during which he seemed to be struggling. Suddenly he looked up at her. "I wish to tell you as quickly as possible that when I was a boy it was my sole responsibility to feed the baby goats from a bottle containing their mother's milk. On one such occasion I managed to spill the goat's milk down my shirtfront — over which I should have been wearing a smock in the first place. And though I can't tell you why, I was wearing my best shirt: perhaps for the like of that alone I deserved to be punished. I went immediately to the washroom and began to rinse out the milk spots, using a large bar of my mother's soap, which was always in plentiful supply since she made it herself. And as I stood there it struck me — my mother's soap was goat's milk soap, with goat's milk I was trying desperately to erase goat's milk. That something could be its own remedy — though I did not then think in those terms — struck me as a rather serious joke. It was my first occasion of panic."

MOMENTS OF DELIGHT

Once Mary found his shopping list — it was written on a pink slip from one of those rainbow pads: *trout, staplegun, cherries, hammer, ribbon, wire.* "Ah, that summer," he said, "that summer. I sought perfection in all things. When a few groceries were needed I would spend hours devising — then revising — the list. Then in the store I carried it crunched in my hand, filled with an excruciating fear: the fear that others would discover, perhaps in the checkout line, that my list was less perfect than theirs."

AGAIN

On the second occasion of Mary's finding a shopping list — this one pinned under the weight of an extra-large egg snug in its styrofoam socket — the anchorite chanced to see her with it. Peering over her shoulder he read *rhubarb, roses, crab legs, gray socks,* then turned to her and said "Isn't that the fate, Madam, of one destined to think in scraps?" What follows are a few of those scraps, thrown to Mary while she did what few chores needed to be done while tending to the anchorite, who was ailing at that time.

RELIGION

Whatever habit one is most faithful to — whatever one does most, loves best, is their religion. A simple matter of precedence.

PENANCE

Penance is the heart of the matter. Why do any of us live the way we do? It is why I live here, in the middle of nowhere. Precisely, it is the penance for never having sinned.

PRAYER

Can we conceive of a religion without prayer? And what, exactly, is prayer? If I am in prayer I seem to be concentrated. But I seem to be concentrating now and I am certainly not in prayer. What then is peculiar to one's concentration in prayer? It seems, simply, that one must concentrate on something that doesn't exist, as in prayers to our Lord, or prayers for the future — prayers for a turn of events, against all odds. What counts is that it does not exist. In which case, algebra seems a very good way to get to heaven.

AN ASIDE

It would be best if one could not hear oneself pray, since one always tends to eavesdrop on their own conversations with God, as though neither of the parties were oneself.

HANDS

It is true I once spent some time in a novitiate. One evening after supper there was a lively conversation concerning whether the ideal hands for prayer should be gloved or ungloved. I suggested that they be disembodied.
"Do you yourself pray — now?" Mary asked.
"My hands pray."
"And what do they pray for?"
"My hands pray to be kept on!"

FAITH OF THE LEGGED

What is the fascination, throughout history, with birds? Is it that they cannot fall? It is just this that the legged envy. If no bird was ever known to sing a song, what difference would be had, since the legged can sing as well? But only the legged can fall. Perhaps the legged sing because they can fall, and the birds sing because they cannot fall, and the fascination with birds, throughout history, is a difference in causation of song. In which case I see that I was not originally wrong. You see, Mary, despite the fact I am legged and can fall, I am never wrong.

HIS TATTOO

Mary noticed a small door, slightly ajar, etched on the left side of his chest.

HIS MOTTO

"I disappear."
Mary learned the anchorite was a great believer in mottoes. He dreamt of a world in which mottoes were given in place of names. In such a world, the mere presentation or introduction of one person to another would result in effortless conversation:
> "Capable of Dissembling"
> "I build"
> "Free from all pastimes"
> "With honor and valor"
> "I disappear"

MARY'S MOTTO

At the the end of the first year of their acquaintance the anchorite gave Mary a motto. It has been a difficult decision, he said, for he wished to bond them through similar mottoes yet bestow Mary with her own characteristics. He finally decided upon "I disappoint."

ON SEX

Just as one lover can be better than another it seems possible that one celibate might be . . . more accomplished . . . than the next. In this vein, I consider myself the greatest of all celibates.

NEWS

"Look here," the anchorite said one day, "I have been reading about a new abyss."
"What's that?" asked Mary.
"The Eucharist is acidic and will upset an ulcer."

SUNDAY PAPER

One Sunday in June he was reading the book review and noticed an author's query, "I would be grateful for information on the life and work of the Spanish painter Maruja Mallo (1902-95)." He thought he would submit an author's query himself, asking gratefully for any information others might have pertaining to his own life and work, giving his own name and the date of his birth. In this way he thought he could learn a good deal more about himself than he already knew, for recent events had led him to realize he was not so well-informed as he had imagined. Proof of this, he told Mary, was the fact he could not even say what these recent events were.

SHAKESPEARE

In the same newspaper he saw an ad for *The Complete Penguin Shakespeare* and he thought it very odd that penguins would bother to read Shakespeare at all.

INCOGNITO

Some of us are happy living a double life, and some of us are tortured by it — though for those there is always the hope that our doubleness will consist in being both of these persons.

CONVERSION

The anchorite ate a single fried egg each morning, just as the sun came up. One morning, while seasoning his egg, he told Mary how he had come to have faith: he simply realized that he had never — not once — refilled his salt and pepper shakers, which he had used profusely for twenty years.

RESPONSIBILITY

God is a toddler. He is learning to walk, tumbling into everything, touching the luminous red surface, surface of your innermost thoughts like coils on a hotplate. He has got to learn. It is up to you to teach him.

HOMUNCULUS

I believe it was Chekhov who said there should be a little man with a hammer in the heads of happy persons, to remind them of the poor and famished. A noble thought . . . but the little man is also a member of the Guilt Berets, and the spiritually fortified should be able to be happy in the midst of great squalor, disappointment, and the most ghastly circumstances. Thus the homunculus must be shot.

IMPERSONAL PROBLEMS

Sometimes I think I am of a species that is bored to extinction, or that I am the last of such a species whose predominant trait was boredom. Nothing modern mind you — not in the least. Just an oversized head that looks up as soon as it gets dark and is heard to remark "Heigh-ho little moon, heigh-ho!". Wherein completes the activity of an evening.

ON WOMEN

I met a twenty-first century French feminist literary critic who said "How can women describe their feelings in a language that was primarily devised by men to describe theirs?". I told her the truth — that that was a direct quote from Thomas Hardy.

LARGE, SAD NUMBERS

Which number is greater — the number of poems collected and preserved by man, or the number of poems thrown away by the women who wrote them? And if the lesser poems outnumber the greater poems, consider this: is it sadder to read such poems or to write them?

TRICK OR TREAT

My head is like a pumpkin with eyes; both hollow and lit. Hollow except for a few seeds, left over from my birth, and long bits of stringy, mashed flesh — yet someone, who is most definitely not myself, has placed a candle there. It positively glows.

HOW FINELY WE ARGUE UPON MISTAKEN FACTS!

ON PRIVACY

Imagine the man who, after having made the world, consented to become a carpenter! I'm led to believe there was a want of privacy. In other words, I'm led to believe there is absolutely no substitute for a human lifetime.

THE MAGNIFYING GLASS

Mary noticed the anchorite did not wear spectacles, nor was there any evidence of such a need. But one large magnifying glass he did keep, and used to distinguish anything he himself had put to ink. "Can't you read your own writing?" she asked, pointing to the magnifying glass. "Oh, that," he said, "it's because my thoughts are so small."

BOOKS

I've read a few, but as for scholars, professors, intellectuals, academics, authors and poets, historians and philosophers — now there's a lot I can't get close to. Their lives would not exist without their books. How they must suffer from an overdose of masterpieces! My idea is . . . memorize as much as you can and forget the rest. Heigh-ho little moon!

ON POETRY

Poets are so coarsely bred they believe in force-feeding, arranged marriages, predestined outbursts. Any two tricks between words will do. It's true, I, too, delight in being vulgar. Yet once I was a boy of five years and one place, I didn't even know the word Poetry existed; I had never read a poem: what did I do then? I went fishing! I lived in a trout's world, that strange underwater adagio. A slow circle. And now I think of it . . . so poetically! Haven't I then been two completely different persons? And lived in at least two worlds? China trees, cinnamon trees, cypress and spindle-wood, the ash tree and the holly bush: some dog has shat on them all. The true trouble with poetry is simple: it depends on distraction to survive. And if God is a poet then I *am* afraid — for it is frightening to think that He is a no one, and speaks not from Himself, but from the character He has found in me.

ART HISTORY

In Bruges, in the 18th century, they sold the shutters of a triptych by Gerard David at the request of the sacristan, who objected to the trouble of opening and closing them, complaining that they broke the altar candles each time he did so. Wise man.

FAVORITE PRAYER

Lord, let nothing get behind me.

DARK MOOD

In a dark mood, I lie down on the ground and the sun that has reached the earth and sunk into it rises up through the ground and enters my back. Nothing comes from above.

TIME TRAVEL

To be transposed to ancient Egypt! It would be like opening the door to my own home, for theirs was a great culture, entirely dedicated to pretending to be dead.

DREAM

A very old librarian with the kind of blue eyes that absorb nothing but reflect everything. The kind you cannot look at, the blueblind eyes of a psychic or beauty queen. She had skin like a fine handkerchief that has been folded many times, smelled faintly of talcum, and wore a rhinestone flower on her lapel. She was in fact the world's expert on violets. She was very sweet to me and gave me a tour of the library which lasted from sunrise to sunset — that's how large the library was. She listened politely while I explained to her that I was only an anchorite with a very small IQ and could not possibly read all the books in her library or even understand them and that the tour, though finely given, had somewhat depressed me. I felt she had wasted her time, and I was sorry. She was even more polite, and infinitely sweeter, when she explained my mistake. These are the books, she said, that have yet to be written, how could anyone read them?

SEQUEL TO A DREAM

The very next night the librarian came back to me, for she had forgotten to tell me something of the utmost importance. She said violets are more common in English literature than the rose, a little known fact that was nonetheless true, and if I thought about this bit of information for long enough it was the equivalent of reading all the books in any earthly library and all those in her own. She told me this with great tact and compassion, as if offering me a little aspirin in the palm of her hand.

INTELLECTUAL FATE

Once I was face to face with a great snowy owl. As

it happened I said to myself this will never happen again. Such a sad reaction! The bird flew off before I could have any other. This is an example of my intellectual fate. I have no memory of the bird whatsoever, and it never happened again.

ON BEARS

The anchorite wanted most to know what the bear felt like upon first awakening from his hibernation. When Mary asked him to elaborate he replied, "That is precisely the question I have in mind: is it an elaborate moment for the bear, or is it essentially spare? Anchored and massive, or does he feel — wouldn't it be delightful — like a fly in a cathedral?"

ON CANCER

We are the brain tumor of the earth. Because of us she wanders the universe with a shaved head, full of spleen, without a cure. One day she will lose the words for *white hawthorn*, *black locust*, *Dutch elm*. Then *periwinkle* will be gone. She will, undoubtedly, still spin. The sound of a Coke bottle being opened on the next planet will bring some momentary sense into her days: she will remember the word for *fizz*. And when she dies, who will be seen squinting at her grave?

ON SYMBOLS

"I don't know of any," he said.

AGE

How odd the years are. If we were thermometers no one would want to be 30; everyone would want to be 78.

PAST LIVES

I am reasonably assured that I was Philip the Assured, who in 1467 was the richest prince in Europe and shut himself up in a little workshop to spend his remaining days fitting together pieces of broken glass. They buried him in St. Donatian's and so great was the throng at his funeral, and the heat engendered by thousand of candles, that they shattered the gorgeous stained glass windows to let in air.

GIFT

Mary asked about the fig tree in his garden. "It was a gift," he said, "from, shall we say, an anchoress I once knew. I dare say she knew exactly what she was presenting me with: the fig tree, as you know, has had an illustrious past: Buddha attained enlightenment under its kin, while Jesus made one barren. Have I then been blessed or cursed?"

BONSAI

Though sometimes it is simple, it is never easy —

to be alone and thinking of nothing. In the bonsai brain, there is no branch so old, and none so small, that from time to time it doesn't do something peculiar!

THE PICKING

I picked a bouquet of twenty lady's slippers, the genitalia of spring, which are an endangered species in these parts. They sat on my desk in a paper cup and gave me great joy. The following year our spring woods, devoid of any such mauve, gave me an even greater thrill.

FAVORITE NOVEL

The book whose every page is turned by Satan's breath! The most ill-mannered, violent, demented book ever written — and by a lady! Can you guess? No, Mary, you're much too dull to know I mean *Wuthering Heights*. And need I remind you of the opening lines of Chapter Ten: "A charming introduction to a hermit's life! Four weeks' torture, tossing, and sickness!"

DECONSTRUCTION

I think the sirens in *The Odyssey* sang *The Odyssey*, for there is nothing more seductive, more terrible, than the story of our own life, the one we do not want to hear and will do anything to listen to.

ONE BOOK

How many books have I read? Only one — just as anyone who is literate has read only one book, or, to be precise, is in the process of reading the one book they will complete in their lifetime. That book is the particular sum of every book they have ever read, written in the particular order in which those books were read. The book is never the same, for no two persons have ever read exactly the same books in exactly the same order. There is a great difference between *The Secret of Larkspur Lane* followed by *Anna Karenina* and *Anna Karenina* followed by *The Secret of Larkspur Lane*. And if *What One Can Do With a Chafing Dish* happens to fall between . . . as opposed to *Don Quixote* . . . well, I don't mean to insult the genetic researchers, but I have a hunch that if no two people are alike, this is why.

ILLITERATES

There are no illiterates! What you call an illiterate is simply someone who has had the time to read the greatest books of all — a bush, a bird, a toe, a star — so that the same principle of a single book applies. The difference you seek is between those who don't understand what they read, and those who do. Now I ask you, to which of these persons does the greatest pleasure belong? That is the interesting question.

EXCEPTION

Why is it we speak of unreliable narrators, but not of unreliable readers? A reader freely judges the author, but the author is not allowed to judge the reader. Except, of course, in the Bible.

WORST YEARS

Mary asked which were the worst years of his life. "Well, there have been two *bad* years — 1951 and 1976. Particularly dry springs — no morels, my dear."

LATE-BREAKING NEWS

My latest occasion of panic was not so far removed from the goat's milk episode of my youth; ten days ago I realized I was sobbing in a Saab.

IT MAY BE

It may be, in an occasional pew, wisdom independent of thought arises: you ought to think deeply about this. There are not, as I once thought, a variety of ways in which we think. I began to worry that I was thinking less and fantasizing more. Until I realized that all thinking is fantasy — the reductionist, structuralist, logician, the computer and the dreamer . . . they are all fantasizing!

END RESULT

You should know there have been several opinions as to what makes the homo sapien distinct. But I think these can be safely reduced to three: his ability to think symbolically, his ability to be bored, and the capacity, in all ages and in all places, for intoxication: corn, palm, sugarcane, vine, curl of the tobacco leaf, poppy unfurled! The holy trinity of what makes man man, woman woman: isn't it sad and ridiculous that according to such criteria the classic human being would be the bored drunk writing poetry? And if I may carry the results further we may distill the distinctions to poetry alone, symbolic thinking which first intoxicates and then bores.

REGRETS

That I am not an electron — lightest of all particles — lightest and lightest of mass — and still to be!

LIVES OF SAINTS AND SAILORS

If people want to touch my body after I am dead, I ask that they refrain from such shameful activity. However, they may kiss the back of my neck as many times as they want, after I am dead, in token of the fact they did not do this to me while I was living.

ON BURIAL

There are only two tombs: the tomb of Jesus and the tomb of Tut. Roll away one stone and you will be given everything: food, clothing, shelter, gems, cloth, seeds and oil, a replica of the world in pure gold. Roll away the other stone and there's nothing.

ACKNOWLEDGMENTS

Thanks to the editors of the following journals, in which many of these pieces first appeared: *The Alaska Quarterly Review*, *Blue Mesa Review*, *Conjunctions*, *Cue*, *Harper's*, *The Iowa Review*, *jubilat*, *The Mississippi Review*, *The Seneca Review*, *Sentence*, *The Southern Review*, *Spoon River Poetry Review*, *Third Coast*, and *TriQuarterly*.

"The Bench" appears courtesy of Carnegie Mellon University Press.

"A Romantic Poet and His Destiny" is slightly altered from a text I found on a paper placemat in a diner off Interstate 91. The poet described is Heinrich Heine (1797-1856). I was served a hamburger on top of this, and had to ask the waitress for a clean "copy" of the mat. I have no idea who wrote it, but I admired its succinctness, for I happened to be reading a five-hundred-page biography of Heine.